THANK YOU FOR BEING YOU!

A LETTER TO MY DAUGHTER

Story By Ambar Gingerelli

Art By Michelle Lubin

LUMINARE PRESS

WWW.LUMINAREPRESS.COM

Illustrations by Michelle Lubin

Luminare Press
442 Charnelton St.
Eugene, OR 97401
www.luminarepress.com

LCCN: 2021918615
ISBN: 978-1-64388-688-6

For my daughter, June.

I am so grateful to be your mom.
Thank you for being you.
You inspire me to be my best me.

MY DAUGHTER, I WANT TO THANK YOU
FOR SO MANY WONDROUS THINGS

YOU'VE OPENED UP MY LIFE
TO ALL THE GIFTS THAT MOTHERHOOD BRINGS

THANK YOU FOR BEING CURIOUS
I SEE THE WORLD THROUGH YOUR EYES

YOU SHOW ME HOW TO BE PRESENT
HOW EACH MOMENT'S A SWEET SURPRISE

THANK YOU FOR BEING PASSIONATE
FOR SHARING JUST HOW YOU FEEL

YOU SHOW ME NO MATTER MY MOOD
WHAT'S IMPORTANT IS TO BE REAL

THANK YOU FOR BEING FRIENDLY
YOU HELP US BOTH MAKE NEW FRIENDS

YOU SPREAD YOUR LOVE AND JOY
AND OUR FUN NEVER ENDS

THANK YOU FOR JUST BEING YOU
YOU BRING OUT MY OWN INNER CHILD

YOUR SENSE OF WONDER IS A BLESSING
YOU HELP ME LET LOOSE AND BE WILD

THANK YOU FOR BEING FEARLESS
YOU INSPIRE ME TO STAND FOR WHAT'S RIGHT

YOU'RE STRONG WILLED AND YOU'RE DETERMINED
YOU TEACH ME TO STAY STRONG AND FIGHT

THANK YOU FOR
BEING FUNNY
YOU REMIND ME TO
STOP AND PLAY

YOU MAKE ME LAUGH
AND GIGGLE

AND KEEP ALL MY
WORRIES AWAY

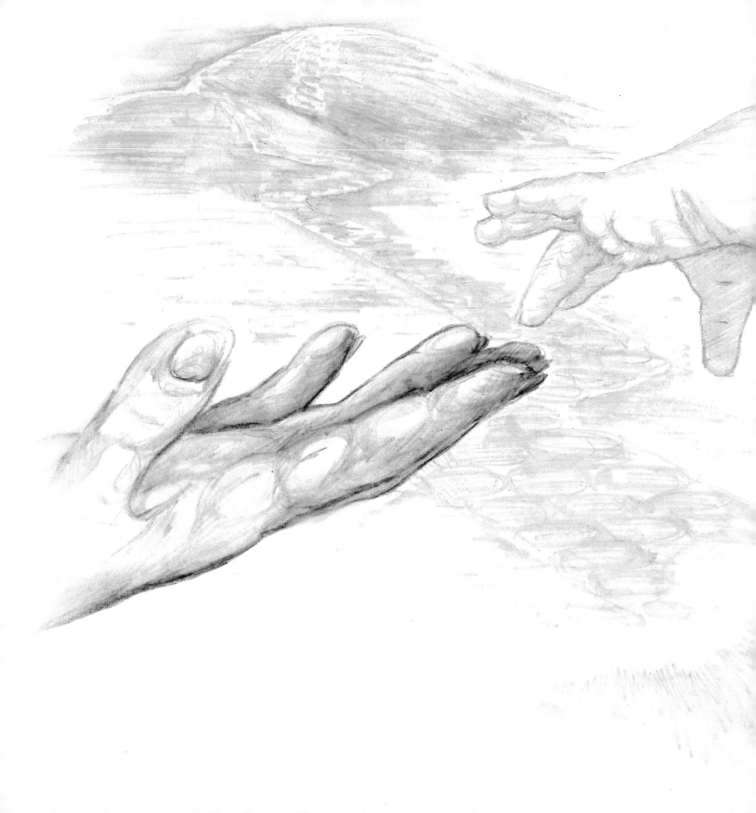

THANK YOU FOR BEING CHARMING
YOU TEACH ME TO DELIGHT WITH A SMILE

I'M GRATEFUL THAT YOU ARE HELPFUL
NOW I'LL GO THE EXTRA MILE

THANK YOU FOR BEING ACTIVE
YOU KEEP ME ON THE MOVE

PLAYING, JUMPING, DANCING
TOGETHER WE FIND OUR GROOVE

THANK YOU FOR BEING BRAVE
YOU INSPIRE ME TO FACE MY FEAR

YOU ALWAYS SPEAK THE TRUTH
REMINDING ME TO BE SINCERE

THANK YOU FOR BEING PRECIOUS
YOU'RE A TREASURE FROM ABOVE

YOUR SWEET AND LOVEABLE SPIRIT
FILLS MY HEART WITH LOVE

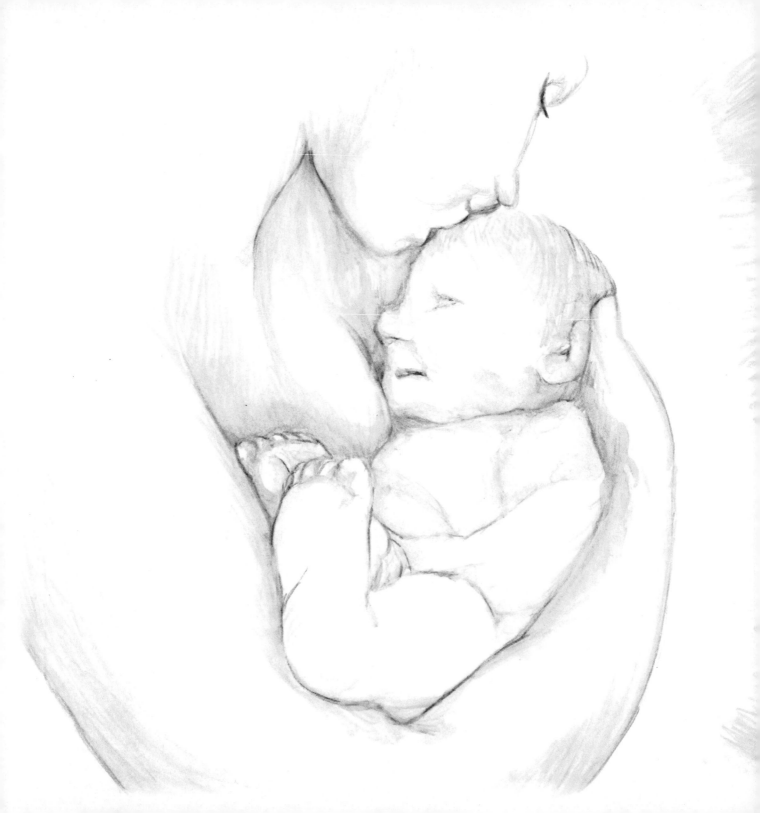

THANK YOU FOR BEING MY DAUGHTER
AND MAKING ME YOUR MOM

OUR CONNECTION IS SO SPECIAL
OUR BOND A WONDERFUL ONE

THANK YOU FOR
BEING MY TEACHER
YOU MAKE ALL MY
LEARNING SO FUN

WE'VE SHARED SO MANY
LESSONS ALREADY

AND OUR JOURNEY HAS
JUST BEGUN

MY DAUGHTER, I WANT TO THANK YOU
FOR SO MANY WONDROUS THINGS

YOU'VE OPENED UP MY LIFE
TO ALL THE GIFTS THAT MOTHERHOOD BRINGS

ABOUT THE AUTHOR

AMBAR GINGERELLI is a writer and life coach. As a new mom, she created the popular blog Mama Bird Well Nest to support mothers through the ups and downs of motherhood. Ambar specializes in helping women decrease stress so that they can take good care of themselves and their families. Ambar lives at the Jersey shore with her husband, Angelo, and daughter, June. *Thank You For Being You* is her first children's book; it was inspired by the many lessons she learns from her daughter everyday. You can connect with Ambar at www.ambargingerelli.com or on Instagram at @mamabirdwellnest.

ABOUT THE ILLUSTRATOR

MICHELLE LUBIN is a Southern California-based visual artist, muralist, and illustrator. When not exhibiting in galleries or painting another "kindness" themed mural in her beach town, Michelle can be found "arting" alongside her daughter, Ava. Inspired by Ava's colorful imagination, the empowering lives and stories of mothers and daughters close to the artist, and of course the touching letter from Ambar to her own daughter, each illustration in *Thank You for Being You* flowed naturally for Michelle. As a female artist, mother, and advocate for mental health awareness, her mission is to ensure a hopeful and healthy future for the next generation of rebel girls and powerful females utilizing creative outlets.

FOR FREE GIFTS
AND RESOURCES VISIT:
AMBARGINGERELLI.COM/TYFBY

Made in the USA
Middletown, DE
02 December 2021